The Happy Troll

Max Bolliger

illustrated by Peter Sís

*Translated from the German
by Nina Ignatowicz*

Henry Holt and Company
New York

Henry Holt and Company, LLC
Publishers since 1866
115 West 18th Street
New York, New York 10011
www.henryholt.com

Henry Holt is a registered trademark of Henry Holt and Company, LLC
Text copyright © 1983, 1998 by Max Bolliger
Illustrations copyright © 1983, 1998, 2005 by Peter Sís
Translation copyright © 2005 by Henry Holt and Company
All rights reserved. Distributed in Canada by H. B. Fenn and Company Ltd.
First published in the United States by Henry Holt and Company, LLC
Originally published in Switzerland in 1983 by Bohem Press under the title *Eine Zwergengeschichte.*

Library of Congress Cataloging-in-Publication Data
Bolliger, Max.
[Zwergengeschichte. English]
The happy troll / by Max Bolliger; translated from the German by Nina Ignatowicz;
illustrated by Peter Sís.—1st American ed.
p.   cm.
Originally published in Switzerland in 1983 by Bohem Press under the title: Eine Zwergengeschichte.
Summary: Gus, a troll who loves to sing, makes everyone happy with his songs until his desire for gold
becomes so strong that he no longer has time to use his beautiful voice.
ISBN-13: 978-0-8050-6982-2
ISBN-10: 0-8050-6982-8
[1. Trolls—Fiction. 2. Singing—Fiction. 3. Greed—Fiction.] I. Ignatowicz, Nina. II. Sís, Peter, ill. III. Title.
PZ7.B635915Hap 2005   [E]—dc22   2004008984

First American Edition—2005 / Designed by Patrick Collins
The artist used oil pastel on gesso to create the illustrations for this book.
Printed in the United States of America on acid-free paper. ∞

1 3 5 7 9 10 8 6 4 2

Once there was a troll.
He was not especially good-looking,
nor was he especially ugly.
He was just an ordinary troll.
His name was Gus.

And like every troll,
Gus had a special talent
that no other troll had.
He had a beautiful voice.

With this voice,
Gus sang not only songs
he had learned from old trolls,
but also songs he composed himself.

In the beginning,
only the children in the neighborhood
came to listen.
But soon trolls came from far and wide
to hear Gus sing.
His singing made them happy.
To show their gratitude,
they would bring him things he needed—
    fresh water,
    crunchy nuts,
    tender roots,
    and juicy berries.
Once in a while they would bring him
a shiny pebble
from the bottom of the brook.

Gus was happy.

Then one day,
a raven with a gold ring on his claw
flew down.
He, too, had heard about Gus's beautiful voice
and begged him to sing a song.
But all Gus could do was stare
at the raven's gold ring and think,
   If only I had a gold ring,
   my happiness would be complete.

"I will sing for you," Gus told the raven,
"if you give me your gold ring."
The raven took off his ring
and gave it to Gus.

Soon thereafter,
a snake with a golden crown on her head
slithered in.
She, too, had heard about Gus's beautiful voice
and begged him to sing a song.
But all Gus could do was stare
at the golden crown and think,
   If only I had a golden crown,
   my happiness would be complete.

"I will sing for you," Gus told the snake,
"if you give me your golden crown."
The snake took off her crown
and gave it to Gus.

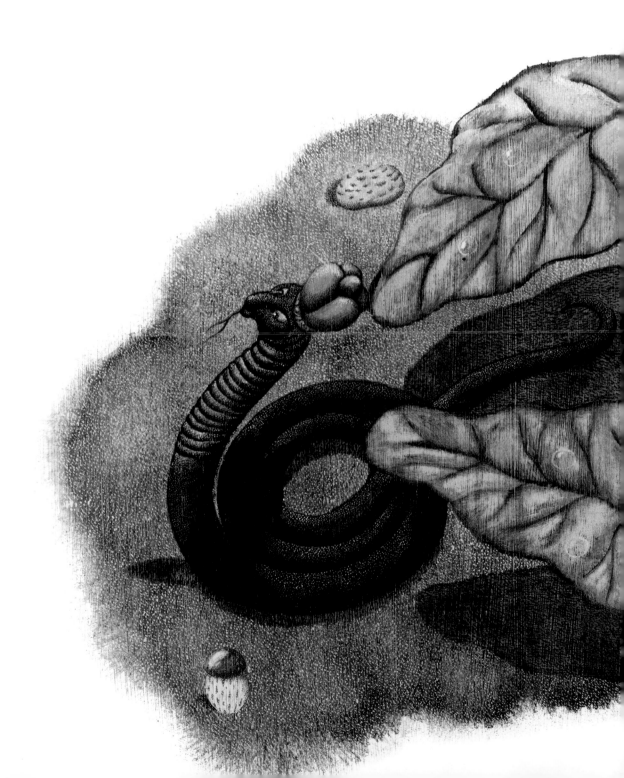

Last to come was a frog.
He drove up in a golden carriage.
He, too, had heard about Gus's beautiful voice
and begged him to sing a song.
But all Gus could do was stare
at the golden carriage and think,
If only I had a golden carriage,
my happiness would be complete.

"I will sing for you," Gus told the frog,
"if you give me your golden carriage."
The frog hopped out of the carriage
and gave it to Gus.

Every day now, Gus rode around
in his golden carriage,
showing off his golden crown and gold ring.
He had no time
to sing his songs.

In vain the trolls begged him to sing.
But Gus only laughed at them.
After a while they left him alone.
The neighborhood children
no longer gathered around him.

Gus was all alone.

He lost the joy of riding around
in his golden carriage,
showing off his golden crown and gold ring.
He stayed inside his house
and tried to sing.
But his voice had lost its beauty,
and no new songs came to him.

Gus was sad.

So Gus set out to find his songs.
He rode his golden carriage
over hills and valleys
until he finally found the raven
perched high up on a tree.

"Take back your gold ring.
I don't need it anymore.
I am looking for my songs,"
Gus told the raven.
"You will find them," said the raven
and flew off with his ring.

Gus drove on and on,
over hills and valleys,
until he finally found the snake
sunning on a rock.

"Take back your golden crown.
I don't need it anymore.
I am looking for my songs,"
Gus told the snake.
"You will find them," said the snake
and slithered away with her crown.

Gus kept on riding over hills and valleys
until at last he saw the frog
sitting on a lily pad.

"Take back your golden carriage.
I don't need it anymore.
I am looking for my songs,"
Gus told the frog.
"You will find them," said the frog
and drove away in his carriage.

There stood Gus—
  without the ring,
  without the crown,
  without the carriage,
  and without his songs.
He longed to be in his own house
together with the other trolls.

Gus started his long journey home—
walking over hills and valleys.
He was hungry,
he was thirsty,
and his feet hurt.

But with every step he took
on his long journey home,
Gus realized that his beautiful voice
and the forgotten songs
were coming back to him.

At last Gus reached his house.
The trolls were there waiting for him
with all the things he needed—
    fresh water,
    crunchy nuts,
    tender roots,
    and juicy berries.
They even had a beautiful shiny pebble
from the bottom of the brook.

To show his gratitude
Gus sang his found-again songs
in his beautiful voice.

Now everyone was happy.